THE TINY DISCIPLES

Age of the Holy Spirit

May God bless

Nicketa Nevils

Nicketa Nevils

ISBN 978-1-68197-305-0 (Paperback)
ISBN 978-1-68197-306-7 (Digital)

Christian Faith Publishing, Inc.
296 Chestnut Street
Meadville, PA 16335
www.christianfaithpublishing.com

Printed in the United States of America

THE
TINY DISCIPLES

FOREWORD

By

Robert J. Rotola, Senior Pastor, Word of Life Ministries

I was much honored to have been asked to write this foreword for Nicketa Nevils. I was her Pastor for many years and have gotten to know her very well during that time. Nicketa is very qualified to write this children's book since she ran a childcare center for many years, as well as other ventures involving children. Her love for children has been evident in everything she has done for them. Nicketa has also been a faithful leader in her church. She is spiritually mature and has a way of describing spiritual matters in a simplified way so that a child can understand and grow as illustrated by this beautifully written children's book.

I absolutely loved reading this book. This book could easily revolutionize a child's life. Each chapter is a short story written in child like fashion and characters, that communicates important truths of the Bible. The author does an excellent job teaching, not only truths about honesty and being a Good Samaritan etc, but also, about faith and intimacy with the Holy Spirit through the eyes of a child. It causes a child to look at each situation through the eyes of Jesus. This book teaches children that they have Mountain moving faith and access to God's power. Children will see the Holy Spirit as the one who speaks to them and guides them through life. Children who read this book will see the world differently. This book will solidify in a child's mind that "Greater is He who is in me, than He that is in the world." They will realize that God working in them is the majority in every situation.

Children will prize walking by faith. They will know that any obstacle they face cannot stand up to the power of God. Children learn to approach friends lovingly, needs benevolently, and mountains forcefully. This book teaches kids at a young age that the unseen world is actually more tangible than the seen world, and God always sees the cup half full. Love for God, country, church and family will be deposited in your child as they read this book. Every child at home or in a public setting would benefit greatly from this book. They will be stirred up to be leaders as well as servants in God's service.

This author and this book will be a great inspiration to your child and will help your child grow spiritually. It is a fun book, easy to understand, and will motivate your child in such a life changing way. So read it with your child, and watch the amazing way God uses this tool to reach your child in a powerful way. Thank you, Nicketa, for loving children, and for writing such an amazing children's book.

HOLY SPIRIT, HERE I AM

But I tell you the truth: It is for your good that I am
going away. Unless I go away, the Holy Spirit will not
come to you: but if I go, I will send him to you.

—John 16:7

Over two thousand five hundred years later, a young boy named Peter was sitting in his living room. He heard a man on television say, "The Holy Spirit is on the earth with us. Call on him, he will help you."

Peter asked his mother, "Mom, who is the Holy Spirit? Is he on the earth?"

Mom said, "Peter, the Holy Spirit is the Spirit of God. The Holy Spirit is good. He will guide us into all truth. He will comfort us also."

Peter said, "Mom, where is the Holy Spirit?"

Mom said, "The Holy Spirit is everywhere. Just call his name, and he will be there."

Peter said, "Just call his name?"

"Yes," said mother.

Peter said, "How will I know him? How will I know he is there?"

Mother said, "The Holy Spirit is a good spirit. He will reveal himself to you in a special way. The Spirit may whisper in your ear. He may touch

1

your heart. The Holy Spirit may talk to you in your mind, or he may talk to you in a dream."

"When John the Baptist, baptized Jesus, the heavens opened, and the Spirit of God descended like a dove upon Jesus. That's from Matthew 3:16," said mother. "Just call his name—Holy Spirit!—when you need help. Have faith."

"I will, said Peter.

Peter went outdoors to play with his puppy named Zoomer. Now Zoomer was fast. Zoomer would dart this way, then dart in the other direction and jump up and down. Peter loved Zoomer, and Zoomer loved Peter. Peter taught Zoomer how to fetch a ball or a stick. Peter would say, "Zoomer, Zoomer, get the ball!" and Zoomer would retrieve the small yellow ball.

Peter and Zoomer were playing ball in the park. Peter threw the ball a long way out, away went Zoomer after the ball.

Peter waited for Zoomer, but no Zoomer came back. Peter yelled, "Zoomer! Zoomer!" But there was no Zoomer. Peter started walking and walking, and then he ran, yelling, "Zoomer, where are you! I can't find you!"

Peter's heart started beating faster and faster. Peter started to cry. He said, "I don't know what to do." Just then, a small voice whispered to him in his ear. The voice sounded like his mother. The voice said, "Call the Holy Spirit."

Peter with tears in his eyes said, "Holy Spirit, I need you. Help me find Zoomer, please."

No sooner than Peter finished praying, Zoomer came running from under a bush, with the yellow ball in his mouth.

"Zoomer! Zoomer!" called Peter. Peter was happy and relieved.

Peter said, "Thank you, Holy Spirit. Thank you."

Study Questions

1. Name the characters in the story.

2. Where did the story take place?

3. How did Peter's mom describe who the Holy Spirit is and what he does?

4. When John baptized Jesus, the Holy Spirit descended on Jesus like a what?

5. What is the name of Peter's dog?

6. What did Peter ask the Holy Spirit to do?

THE MISSION

The missionary said to the church audience, "Pray for me as I go forward to do God's will in Africa."

"Dad! Dad!" said Megan as they walked out of the church. What is God's will for the missionary to do in Africa?" asked Megan.

"Well," said Dad, "Sister JoAnn will attend to the needs of the people. She will do the same thing as Jesus did when he walked this earth. Jesus taught the people to know God, he taught the people to pray and how to please God. How to love one another."

"That is a lot to do" said Meagan.

"Yes, it is," said Dad. "That is why Sister JoAnn asked us to pray for her."

"Okay, Dad, I will," said Megan.

At the dinner table, all the conversation was about Sister JoAnn's mission trip to Africa.

"I think it is a wonderful blessing that Sister JoAnn will give her time and effort to hurting people," said Mama.

"God has given Sister JoAnn a good heart and a strong will," said Dad.

Clint, my younger brother, said, "Will she see the animals?"

"I suppose so," said Dad.

That night, Megan dreamed she flew to Esteria, Africa. At the airport, she was met by four other missionaries. We were glad to see one another and gave God the thanks for a good flight.

While in Esteria, Megan worked with the children's mission, she saw herself telling the children about Jesus. Megan said, "Shepherds were watching their sheep. Suddenly a brilliant light filled the sky, and angels appeared.

They told the shepherds where they could find Jesus, the savior who was promised long ago was now born. Then the angels shouted praises to God and disappeared into heaven.

Megan helped feed the babies that were too sick to hold their heads up. Megan also taught the children about prayer. Megan said, "God wants us to talk to him. Prayer is talking to God. You can talk to God anywhere about anything. God always hears and understands." When Megan awoke the next morning, she felt all warm and excited inside.

Today was Thursday. Megan's mom always volunteered at the soup kitchen. "Can I help you today, Mom, at the soup kitchen?" said Megan.

"I don't know, Megan. It is sometimes hard work," said Mom.

"I know," said Megan, "but I want to practice being a missionary."

Study Questions

1. Name the characters in the story.

2. Where did the story take place?

3. Where was Sister JoAnn going? And why?

4. In Megan's dream, what country did she visit in Africa?

5. What jobs did Megan do in her dream?

6. Megan wanted to be a _____.

KICKBALL

"It's your turn," said Stan to James.

"Dear Lord, help me to kick this ball over their heads, landing far into the outer field," said James to himself.

Carla rolled the ball to James. James ran up to the ball and kicked the ball with all his might. The ball went up, up over everyone's head, far into the outer field. James ran to the first base, the second base and stopped on the third base.

"Boy oh boy!" said James to himself. "Thank you, Lord Jesus, for hearing and answering my prayer."

Lenny was next to kick the ball. Carla rolled the ball to Lenny. Lenny kicked the ball with all his strength. The ball went sailing into the air. Lois and Pauline were talking in the outer field, not paying attention to the ball. The ball turned right and hit Pauline in the face. Pauline fell to the ground, unconscious. All the children ran to the area where Pauline laid on the ground. When James reached the area, the Holy Spirit spoke to him.

"You must pray," said the Holy Spirit.

James looked around the crowd of children and saw seven children he knew were believers. "Tiny disciples, stretch out your hands toward Pauline, and repeat after me. Dear Jesus, Pauline is your child, and she is our friend. Please wake her up and make her well, in Jesus's name," said James.

Ms. Peter, the gym teacher, came running and said, "Step aside." Ms. Peter kneeled down and touched Pauline's hand.

"Pauline," said Ms. Peter.

Pauline opened her eyes and smiled at Ms. Peter. All the children jumped and yelled.

"Thank you, Jesus," said James.

Study Questions

1. Name the characters in the story.

2. Where did the story take place?

3. Name the tiny disciple who prayed to Jesus for help to kick the ball over the other children's heads. Did he do it?

4. Name the tiny disciple who got hit in the face with a ball.

5. Name the tiny disciple whom the Holy Spirit spoke to. What did the Holy Spirit say to him?

6. There were seven children James knew who were believers of Christ, what did they do as James prayed for Pauline?

PRACTICING BEING JESUS

Two thousand five hundred years later.

"Nathan," said Ms. Smith, the Sunday school teacher, "who is Jesus?"

"He is the Son of God," said Nathan.

"That is correct," said Ms. Smith. "What miracles did Jesus do while he lived on earth?" said Ms. Smith.

James said, "Jesus healed the sick, he made the lame to walk, and he casted out demons."

"And and Jesus turned water into wine and walked on water," said Marques.

"Jesus also calmed the raging sea," said Susan.

"You are all correct," said Ms. Smith. "Class, do you believe the miracles of Jesus?"

"Yes, yes," said the entire class.

"Class dismissed," said Ms. Smith.

"What a good lesson," said Nathan to James. "Do you believe the word of God?"

"I sure do," said James.

"Good," said Nathan. "Let's meet at my house after lunch and practice."

"Okay," said James. "I will see if Marques can come too."

Nathan's House

James and Marques knocked on Nathan's door. Marquis had his young sister, Nicole, with him.

"Come on in," said Nathan.

Up the stairs went the children. Nathan threw open the door, and the children entered the room with loud praises to Jesus. "Glory to Jesus. Hallelujah. Hallelujah to God in the highest. Reign Lord Jesus forever and ever." They sang the song "Here We Are Jesus, the Tiny Disciples, Here to Do Your Will."

"Jesus healed the sick. Is there anyone here who needs a healing?" said Nathan.

"Yes," said Marques. "My little sister, Nicole, has a bruise on her left leg."

"Okay," said Nathan. "I will lay my hand over her bruise. The rest of you stretch out your hands toward her leg."

James prayed, "Jesus, whom all blessings come from, heal Nicole's leg, make her well, in Jesus's name."

The tiny disciples watched Nathan's hamster run around in his wheel, fed the fishes, and played Bible quiz on the computer the rest of the day.

Study Questions

1. Name the characters in the story.

2. Where did the story take place?

3. When Ms. Smith asked who was Jesus (and what did he do?), what were some of the responses from the tiny disciples?

4. Whose house did the tiny disciples meet at?

5. When the tiny disciples entered Nathan's room, what did they say?

6. Who did the tiny disciples pray for? Why was prayer needed?

THE FIRE

Bruce was awakened by the smell of smoke. When he sat up in his bed, he could hear the smoke alarm and see the smoke.

Bruce said, "Help! Help! Mommy, Mommy! Help me!"

"Bruce, Bruce, Mommy is coming," said Mommy.

"I can't see you, Mommy. I'm scared," said Bruce.

Charles and James heard the siren noise of the fire trucks and the policemen. They ran from their homes in pajamas toward the fire. Annie and Lenny came running also.

"Bruce and his mom are in there," said James.

"What can we do?" said Annie.

Paul, who lived in the neighborhood, ran up to the group of children and said, "Tiny disciples, let's do something."

"Stretch out your hands toward the fire," said James, "and pray for the Holy Spirit to rescue Bruce and his mom."

This was their prayer: "Holy Spirit, Bruce and his mom needs you now. Please rescue them. We all join our faith together in one accord. Save them, save them, in Jesus's name," said the children.

Meanwhile, Bruce, still in his room, felt along the wall and prayed, "Holy Spirit, I need you. I'm afraid. I can't see."

Just then, Bruce saw a hand reach out to him. "Bruce, take my hand," said the voice.

Bruce stretched his hand out to the hand. The hand led Bruce through the smoke, through the fire, down the stairs, through the hallway, where a fireman reached out and grabbed Bruce into his arms.

Bruce's mom was rescued by the firemen also.

Everyone cheered when Bruce and his mother came out of the house.

"Bruce! Bruce! Are you all right?" said the tiny disciples.

"Yes," said Bruce. "The most wonderful thing happened to me. I was afraid, and I prayed for the Holy Spirit to help me. I heard a voice call me by name, and a stretched-out hand lead me through the fire into the arms of a fireman. Look at my clothes. They are not burned."

The tiny disciples looked at one another and stretched their hand toward the sky and sang, "Thank you, Jesus. Thank you, Jesus, for saving our friend."

Study Questions

1. Name the characters in the story.

2. Where did the story take place? What happened?

3. When Paul said, "Let's do something," what did the tiny disciples do?

4. What did Bruce see in his room? What did Bruce hear?

5. Who did Bruce ask to help him?

6. What song did the tiny disciples sing?

THE BOY IN CLASS

"Dad, there is a boy in our class. His clothes are kind of dirty and dingy. His hair has not been cut or combed well," said Carl. "And… and nobody likes to play with him or sit by him. Some people said he smells."

"Carl," said Dad, "let me tell you a story. A certain man entered the church wearing an expensive suit. The man wearing the suit was told, 'Sit here, sir. This is the best seat in the house.' A street man wearing rags also entered the church. He was told to sit in the back. Does God isolate? Is God prejudiced? I should say not. Are you a judge, Carl?"

"No, Dad," said Carl.

"God chooses the world's down-and-out as the first citizens, with full rights and privileges. God's kingdom is promised to everyone who loves Jesus," said Dad.

"I love Jesus," said Carl, "but, Dad, what can I do?"

"Well," said Dad, "you can begin by introducing yourself to the young boy, and do not forget his name. If the young boy plays or eat by himself, invite him to play with you and ask him to sit at your table for breakfast and lunch."

"But, Dad, if I do that, the other children may not want to play with me or want me at their table," said Carl.

"Carl," said Dad, "who do we seek to please? All the other children or God?"

"I want to please God," said Carl.

Study Questions

1. Name the characters in the story

2. Where did the story take place?

3. What did Carl say about the boy in class?

4. Is God prejudice? Should we be prejudice? Does God isolate people?

5. Who did dad say Gods' Kingdom is promised to?

6. Who should we seek to please in this world?

THE TORNADO

The sky was a greenish gray color, with dark clouds. The air smelled of rain and dirt. Suddenly, the wind began to blow softly, then hard.

Ms. Johnson, our teacher, stood looking out the window. She was rubbing her neck up and down with her hand.

"Ms. Johnson," said Joy, "is it going to rain?"

"It looks that way," said Ms. Johnson.

Mr. Lewis, the principal, came to the classroom door and motioned to Ms. Johnson to step outside the door.

The wind blew slowly, then picked up, then slowly, then picked up again, like a toy top. The clouds appeared to be moving while another set of clouds did not move at all.

Ms. Johnson came back into the room.

"Class," said Ms. Johnson, "we are going to our storm shelter until the storm is over."

Lois and Pauline looked at each other.

"I have never been inside the storm shelter at school," said Pauline.

"Neither have I," said Lois.

"I'm afraid," said Pauline.

"Me too," said Lois.

Joy overheard Pauline and Lois's conversation. "The word of God says, 'Let not your heart be troubled, neither be afraid.' Do you believe in the word of God?" asked Joy.

"Yes," said Pauline.

"Yes," said Lois.

"Children, line up in a single line and follow me," said Ms. Johnson.

Joy spotted Butch and Lenny in another line, walking to the storm shelter.

"Don't be afraid," said Lenny to Joy. "The Holy Spirit has spoken to my heart to pray."

"We will all pray said," said Butch.

The children walked through the hallway and down the stairs to the basement. Mr. Lewis told the children to sit along the wall and put their arms over their heads and put their heads down.

"Mr. Lewis, Mr. Lewis, some of the kids would like to pray, please!" said Butch.

Mr. Lewis looked at Butch for a moment. Then he said, "Well, go ahead, but make it quick."

Butch kneeled down and asked everyone to hold hands. Butch recited the Psalms 91:1–16.

He that dwells in the shelter of the Most High
Will rest in the shadow of the Almighty.
I will say of the Lord, "He is my refuge and my fortress,
my God, in whom I trust."

Surely he will save you
from the fowler's snare
and from the deadly pestilence.

He will cover you with his feathers,

And under his wings you will find refuge,

His faithfulness will be your shield and rampart.

You will not fear the terror of night,

Nor the arrow that flies by day,

nor the pestilence that stalks in the darkness,

nor the plague that destroys at midday.

A thousand may fall at your side,

ten thousand at your right hand,

but it will not come near you.

You will only observe with your eyes

and see the punishment of the wicked.

If you say, "The Lord is my refuge,"

And you make the Most High your dwelling,

No harm will overtake you,

no disaster will come near your tent.

For he will command his angels concerning you

To guard you in all your ways;

While Butch was praying, the tornado siren sounded. Butch was somewhat shaken, but he continues to pray.

They will lift you up in their hands,

So that you will not strike your foot against a stone.

You will tread on the lion and the cobra;

you will trample the great lion and the serpent.

"Because he loves me," says the Lord, "I will rescue him;
I will protect him, for he acknowledges my name.
He will call on me, and I will answer him;
I will be with him in trouble,
I will deliver him and honor him.
With long life I will satisfy him
and show him my salvation."

Study Questions

1. Name the characters in the story.

2. Where did the story take place?

3. Where did Ms. Johnson tell the class they were going and why?

4. What did Joy tell Pauline and Lois about the word of God?

5. Who did Lenny say had spoken to his heart? What did the Holy Spirit tell him to do?

6. In Butch's prayer, name the many ways God will protect you.

THE DRAGON SLAYER

"Dad! Dad!" said Alex. "Last night, I had the most wonderful dream."

"Tell me your dream," said Dad.

"I dreamed a voice, a strong but gentle voice, a voice that sounded like it came from many waters in a well, called my name. I found myself walking into an arena, and there was no one there, I thought, until I heard the voice. The voice said, 'Look there.' I looked and there was a small snake on the floor near me. I became afraid and looked for something to kill the snake with. The only thing I saw was a string. The voice said, 'Strike it.' I said, 'What?' The voice said, 'Strike it.' I picked up the string. It was limp and lifeless.

"The voice said again, 'Strike it.' I said, 'With a string?' But I did what I was told. I took the limp string and struck the snake. The snake twisted back and forth, as if the string irritated it. To my amazement, the snake grew larger. I dropped the string, again I looked for something to kill the snake with. The string I had dropped turned into a long pole. I heard the voice. The voice said, 'Strike it.'

"I picked up the pole, and again, I did as I was told. I hit the snake with the pole. The snake twisted and turned as if the pole hurt and angered it. The snake grew larger still. I dropped the pole and inhaled a deep breath. The pole I had dropped turned into a strong iron pipe. The voice said, 'Strike it.' I felt in my body that I was stronger, and I know longer felt afraid. I hit the snake, very hard. The snake twisted and turned. It was very angry and turned into a dragon. The iron pipe I held in my hand turned into a great sword. The voice said, 'Cut the head off.'

"I felt great strength in my body. I was fearless. I took the sword in both hands, and with one strike, I took the dragon's head. I heard many cheers, but I saw no one. To God be the praise and glory forever."

Study Questions

1. Name the characters in the story.

2. Where did the story take place?

3. What did the voice represent?

4. What did the snake represent?

5. Name the instruments Alex used to attack the snake.

6. Alex heard many cheers but saw no one. Who do you think the cheers came from?

THE HOLY SPIRIT DESCENDED

And the Holy Spirit descended on him in bodily form
like a dove. And a voice came from heaven: "you are my
son, whom I love; with you I am well pleased.
—Luke 3:22

It was a warm, sunny, and breezy day. The children were playing in the park. Toya, Megan, Lois, and Pauline were playing in the water fountain. Butch, James, Lenny, and Charles were tossing a softball to each other. Carl and Marquis were playing together on a video game, while Peter, Francine, and Joy played tag. Everyone was laughing and was happy.

All the children heard someone talking loudly.

"Who is that?" said Lenny.

"I don't know," said Butch.

"It sounds like Little Bear," said Francine.

"Let's go and see," said Charles.

All the children stopped what they were doing and followed the sound of the voice.

The Holy Spirit had descended on Little Bear. The children gather around him, sitting on the ground. This is what the Holy Spirit said through Little Bear:

"God, my shepherd!

I don't need a thing

You have bedded me down in lush
meadows,
you find me quiet pools to drink from.
True to your word,
You let me catch my breath
And send me in the right direction.
Even when the way goes through Death Valley,
I'm not afraid, when you walk at my side.
Your trusty shepherd's crook
makes me feel secure.
You serve me a six-course
dinner,
right in front of my enemies:
You revive my drooping head;
My cup brims with blessing.
Your beauty and love chase after me
Every day of my life.

I'm back home in the house of God
For the rest of my life. Amen."

Study Questions

1. Name the characters in this story.

2. Where did the story take place?

3. Name the different games the tiny disciples were playing.

4. All the children heard someone talking loudly. Who was it?

5. The _____ had descended on Little Bear.

6. Name four things the Holy Spirit said through Little Bear.

THE PRAYER LINE

"Good morning parents, boys, and girls. It has been snowing all weekend long, and it's still coming down. The wind is blowing forty-five miles an hour, causing snow drifts and blizzard conditions. The superintendent of schools has cancelled school today for our safety," said the newsman.

"Oh boy!" said Lenny. "No school today. Mom, can I call Butch on the cell phone?"

"I suppose so," said Mom.

"Butch," said Lenny, "have you heard school is out today because of the snow?"

"No, I had not heard," said Butch. "Let's call Marques and hook him into our line."

"You call Marques, Butch, and I will call Joy and hook her in also," said Lenny.

"Okay," said Butch.

"Hello, everyone, school is out today because of blizzard conditions," said Lenny. "I thought I would call each of you so we could get a morning prayer in."

"Sounds good to me," said Joy, "but please, can I call Megan and hook her in?"

"I don't see why not," said Marques.

"Megan," said Joy, "you are on a prayer line this morning with Lenny, Butch, Marques, and I."

"Wonderful," said Megan.

"Let's begin," said Lenny. "Butch, will you take us to the throne of God?"

"Yes," said Butch. "Lord Jesus, watch over the city street workers who are clearing the roads for all of our safety. Send angels to help all travelers who may be caught in the snow. Amen."

"Joy," said Lenny, "you're next."

"Thank you, Lord, for waking me up this morning," said Joy. "Dear Lord, take care of all the birds and all animals outdoors. Please feed them and keep them warm. Amen."

"Marques, you are next," said Lenny.

"God is great and greatly to be praised," said Marques. "Lord Jesus, take care of all the first responders, cover them and protect them from harm. Lord, protect our power lines. Do not let them snap. Let no tree limbs break and fall on our houses or our automobiles. Amen."

"It is your turn now, Megan," said Lenny.

"The Lord is my shepherd," said Megan. "Jesus, watch over the mailmen. Please bless their feet. Do not let them slip down. Bless all the doctors, nurses, and all hospital personnel. Keep them all safe so they can take care of the needs of the patients. Amen."

"Bless the Lord all my soul and all that is within me, bless his Holy name," said Lenny. "This is the day the Lord has made. Let us rejoice and be glad in it. Thank you, Lord, although it is snowing outside, our homes are nice and warm. Do not let our gas lines freeze, dear Lord. You have blessed our refrigerators and cabinets to be full of good food to eat. Bless our waterlines not to freeze, so we will have water to drink. Thank you, Father, for Christian friends, who love you and like to pray. Amen."

Study Questions

1. Name the characters in the story.

2. Where does the story take place?

3. Why are the tiny disciples at home?

4. What means did the tiny disciples use to communicate with each other?

5. Name the tiny disciples who prayed for the first responders.

6. Name the tiny disciples who thanked God for Christian friends.

MIRACLE IN A POT

Today Megan and Lois accompanied their mothers to the soup kitchen.

"Megan," said her mother, "you and Lois go wash your hands, put on a hair net, your gloves, and aprons."

Butch, James, and Lenny came into the kitchen with Pastor Moore. Carl came into the kitchen with his dad.

Pastor Moore said, "To all the volunteers, gather around for prayer. Dear Lord, we are here today to feed the people food and the word of God. Thank you for the opportunity to be a blessing. Bless the food and every volunteer. In Jesus's name. Now let's get to your stations, and have a blessed day."

Carl said to Lenny as they were putting on their aprons, "Lenny did you see all the people?"

"I sure did," said Lenny.

"Carl, I need your help over here with the rolls," said Dad.

"Okay," said Carl.

"Megan, Lois, and Butch, wipe all the tables off," said Lois's mother.

"James and Lenny, report to the soup station," said Pastor More.

Mr. Parker is over the soup station. "Lenny, get my largest pot out, and put it on the stove," said Mr. Parker. "James, you will find one hundred gallons of beef stew in the walk-in refrigerator. Let's start with fifty gallons of soup."

"Right away," said James.

"Lenny, start pouring the soup into the pot," said Mr. Parker.

"Okay," said Lenny.

"Megan, Lois, and Butch report to the desert station," said Megan's mother.

Carl put trays of rolls on the serving table. James left the soup area briefly to help put plastic ware out.

"Five minutes and we open the doors," said Pastor Moore.

James returned to the soup area and started filling bowls with soup. Lenny would set the bowls of soup in the service window.

The doors to the soup kitchen were open. The people filtered in.

"Here they come," said Lois.

"I'm ready,'" said Carl.

The people kept coming and coming. Butch, Lois, and Megan worked between cleaning tables and keeping the desert station filled with plenty of deserts.

Lenny and James kept busy in the soup area.

"James," said Mr. Parker, "get thirty more gallons of soup from the refrigerator.

"Right away," said James.

Pastor Moore and the other ministers visited with the people. There was a steady flow of people coming into the soup kitchen. The little disciples took a break.

"Wow," said Carl, "the people are still coming in."

"I'm getting tired," said Lois.

"So am I," said Meagan.

"Tiny disciples, let us do this work unto the Lord," said Lenny.

"We will pray our strength in the Lord," said James.

James and Lenny returned to the soup area.

"James," said Mr. Parker, "get the remaining twenty gallons of soup from the refrigerator."

"Okay, Mr. Parker," said James.

"Mr. Parker," said Lenny, "what happens if this is not enough soup to feed the people?"

"Well, boys, we pray," said Mr. Parker.

James and Lenny looked at each other.

"Are you thinking what I'm thinking?" said Lenny.

"If you are thinking to pray over the soup, I am," said James.

Lenny prayed, "Lord Jesus, we know that nothing is too hard for you. You fed five thousand people with only five loaves of bread and two fishes. James and I are asking you to bless this soup to feed your people, again. Amen."

The soup in the pot started getting low, then very low.

"I have faith in the word of God," said Lenny.

"I do too," said James.

"We have about fifty more people left," said Pastor Moore.

"Fifty more people!" said James. "Just keep on dipping in the pot for soup," said Lenny.

James kept dipping soup, and Lenny kept fixing bowls of soup.

"Hey, James," said Lenny, "the pot should have been empty an hour ago."

"I felt the same," said James.

"That's it, everyone. We have fed the last person. Good job, everyone," said Pastor Moore.

James and Lenny looked inside the soup pot, and there was more soup in the pot.

"Thank you, Jesus, for the miracle in the pot," said Lenny.

Study Questions

1. Name the characters in the story.

2. Where did the story take place?

3. Name the different jobs the tiny disciples performed.

4. Name three things Pastor Moore prayed for.

5. In Lenny's prayer, what did he ask Jesus to do?

6. What was the miracle in the pot?

ABOUT THE AUTHOR

Nicketa Nevils has been around children all her life. The oldest of seven siblings. A Sunday school teacher, worked as a paraprofessional at a Special Purpose School for handicapped children and was past president of Genesis 3 Inc. (a not for Profit children organization), director of Play Time at Billies Child Care Center, a substitute teacher in the public school system, and a minister of the Gospel of Jesus Christ for twenty years.

Nicketa Nevils is happily married and deeply devoted to her husband, Rev. James Nevils, and daughters, Nicole, Myrisha, LeAnn, and Frances, who are a constant source of love and support.

CPSIA information can be obtained
at www.ICGtesting.com
Printed in the USA
FSOW04n2321240717
36532FS